Topsy and Tim
Meet the Firefighters

By Jean and Gareth Adamson

Illustrations by Belinda Worsley

A catalogue record for this book is available from the British Library

This title was previously published as part of the Topsy and Tim Learnabout series
Published by Ladybird Books Ltd
A Penguin Company
Penguin Books Ltd., 80 Strand, London WC2R 0RL, UK
Penguin Books Australia Ltd., Camberwell, Victoria, Australia
Penguin Group (NZ) 67 Apollo Drive, Rosedale, North Shore 0632, New Zealand (a division of Pearson NZ Ltd)

001 –
1 3 5 7 9 10 8 6 4 2

© Jean and Gareth Adamson MMVII
This edition MMXI

ISBN: 978-1-40930-721-1
Printed in China

www.topsyandtim.com

This Topsy and Tim book belongs to

_____

One morning, when Topsy and Tim were on their way to school, they heard a fire engine coming.

It raced past them, sirens sounding and blue lights flashing. All the other traffic got out of the way. Everyone knew that the firefighters were hurrying to put out a fire.

"Kerry's dad is a firefighter," said Topsy.
"I expect he is on that fire engine."

But Kerry's dad was not on the fire engine. It was his morning off and he was taking Kerry to school. Topsy and Tim told him about the fire engine they had seen.

"They're called fire appliances, not fire engines," said Kerry.

"There's an open day at my fire station on Saturday,"
said Kerry's dad. "Would you like to come and see all
our fire appliances?"
"Yes, please," said Topsy and Tim.
On Saturday, Topsy and Tim and Mummy set out for
Bellford Fire Station.

There were lots of children at the fire station. Firefighters in yellow helmets were looking after them.

Topsy and Tim soon found Kerry and her dad. Kerry was
waiting to go up on a long turntable ladder. Topsy and Tim
wanted to go up too. A firefighter helped them all into a cage
on the end of the ladder. He gave them safety helmets to wear.

A firefighter at the back of the appliance pulled a lever and the ladder started to go up.

It grew longer and longer and went higher and higher, until the people on the ground looked as small as toys. "We hose water down on to burning buildings from up here," said the firefighter. "And you rescue people from high windows and roofs," said Kerry.

When they came down from the ladder, Mummy bought
them each a little firefighter's helmet.

"I'm going to be a firefighter when I grow up," said Kerry.

"Can girls be firefighters?" asked Topsy.

"I don't think so," said Tim.

"Yes, they can!" said the lady who was selling the toy helmets. "I'm a firefighter, just like Kerry's dad. Women can be firefighters, but they have to be as strong and as brave as the men."
To show how strong she was, she gave Tim a fireman's lift.

Kerry's dad took them to see how the fire station worked. "When there is a fire and someone phones 999," he said, "we get the message on a printer. A loudspeaker tells us where to go and which appliances to take."

"Alarm bells ring and the firefighters run to the appliances. If they are upstairs they slide down a pole. It's quicker than running down the stairs."

Kerry's dad lifted the children into the cab of a big fire appliance. They pretended to drive to a fire.

Near the big fire appliance was a much
smaller one.
"Is that a baby fire engine?" asked Tim.
"It's a van full of rescue equipment," said
Kerry's dad. "We take it to accidents and
rescue people from crashed cars and trucks."

Kerry's dad showed them the tall tower where the
firefighters practised with their ladders and hoses.
"When we have finished we hang the hoses in the
tower to dry," he told them.
Next to the tower was a room that had been on fire.
It made their noses tickle.

"We make smoky fires in there," said Kerry's dad. "Then we practise putting them out and rescuing people. We have to wear masks and carry tanks of air on our backs, or we would choke."

Kerry took Topsy and Tim into a showroom full of fire
dangers. It looked like an ordinary living room.
"See if you can spot where fires could start," said Kerry.
Tim spotted an iron that had been left face-down.
"That could start a fire," he said.

Topsy spotted a box of matches on the floor.
"A naughty little child might start a fire with those," she said.
"And that fire should be behind a fireguard," said Mummy.

Mummy spotted more fire dangers near a kitchen
stove. "Are smoke detectors any use?" she asked
Kerry's dad. "I think I ought to get some."
Kerry's dad showed them a smoke detector and made it
work. It made loud *BLEEP-BLEEP-BLEEP* noises.

"If there was a fire in your home one night, the smoke detectors would wake you up," he said.
"We've got some smoke detectors," Kerry told Topsy.

It was time to go home, but before they went, Kerry's dad gave them one last treat. It was a ride round the fire station yard on a children's fire appliance. The clever firefighters had made it specially for their open day, and it went *nee-naw, nee-naw, nee-naw* — just like a real fire engine.

*Now turn the page and help
Topsy and Tim solve a puzzle.*

Follow the hoses and see if you can help Topsy and Tim work out which one is putting out the fire.

A Map of the Village

farm

Topsy and Tim's house

Tony's house

Ker ho

park

garage

post
office

health
centre

church

primary school

nursery school

police station

Look out for other titles in the series.

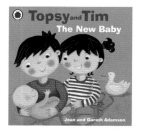
Topsy and Tim — The New Baby
Jean and Gareth Adamson

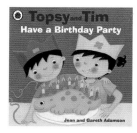
Topsy and Tim — Have a Birthday Party
Jean and Gareth Adamson

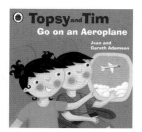
Topsy and Tim — Go on an Aeroplane
Joan and Gareth Adamson

Topsy and Tim — Play Football
Jean and Gareth Adamson

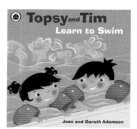
Topsy and Tim — Learn to Swim
Jean and Gareth Adamson

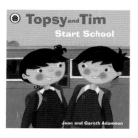
Topsy and Tim — Start School
Jean and Gareth Adamson

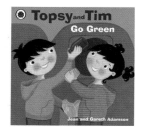
Topsy and Tim — Go Green
Jean and Gareth Adamson

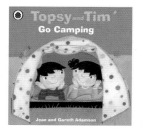
Topsy and Tim — Go Camping
Jean and Gareth Adamson

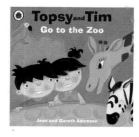
Topsy and Tim — Go to the Zoo
Jean and Gareth Adamson

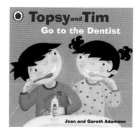
Topsy and Tim — Go to the Dentist
Jean and Gareth Adamson

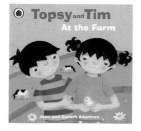
Topsy and Tim — At the Farm
Jean and Gareth Adamson

Topsy and Tim — Go to the Doctor
Jean and Gareth Adamson

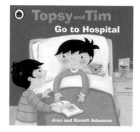
Topsy and Tim — Go to Hospital
Jean and Gareth Adamson

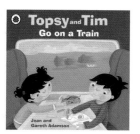
Topsy and Tim — Go on a Train
Jean and Gareth Adamson

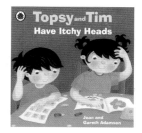
Topsy and Tim — Have Itchy Heads
Jean and Gareth Adamson